STANLEY

and the Magic Lamp

Also by Jeff Brown
Flat Stanley
coming soon
Invisible Stanley

STANLEY
and the Magic Lamp

By Jeff Brown
Illustrated by Steve Björkman

SCHOLASTIC INC.

New York Toronto London Auckland Sydney
Mexico City New Delhi Hong Kong Buenos Aires

For Elizabeth Tobin
—J.B.

CONTENTS

Prologue

Once upon a very long time ago, way before the beginning of today's sort of people, there was a magical kingdom in which everyone lived forever, and anyone of importance was a genie, mostly the friendly kind. The few wicked genies kept out of sight in caves or at the bottoms of rivers. They had no wish to provoke the great Genie King, who ruled from a palace with many towers and courtyards and gardens with reflecting pools.

The Genie King was noted for his patience with the high-spirited genie princes of the kingdom, but the Genie Queen thought he was much *too* patient with them. She said so one morning in the throne room, where the King was studying reports and proposals for new magic spells.

"Discipline, that's what they need!" She adjusted the Magic Mirror on the throne room wall. "Florts and collibots! Granting wishes, which they'll be doing one day, is serious work."

"Florts yourself! You're too hard on the lads," said the King, and then he frowned. "However, this report here says that one of them has been behaving very badly indeed."

"Haraz, right?" said the Queen. "He's a *real* smarty!"

The Genie King sent a thought to summon

Prince Haraz, which is all such a ruler has to do when he wants somebody, and a moment later the young genie flew into the throne room, did a triple flip, and hovered in the air before the throne.

"What's up?" he asked, grinning.

"You are!" said the Queen. "Come down here!"

"No problem," said Haraz, landing.

"It seems you have been playing a great many magical jokes," said the king, tapping the reports before him. "Very *annoying* jokes, such as causing the army's carpets to fly only in circles, which made all my soldiers dizzy."

"That was a good one!" laughed Haraz.

"And turning the Chief Wizard's wand

into a sausage, while he was casting a major spell? You did that?"

"Ha, ha! You should have seen his face!"

"Stop laughing!" cried the Queen. "This is shameful! You should be severely punished!"

"He's just a boy, dear, only two hundred years old," said the King. "But I'll—"

"Who knows what more he's done?" The Queen turned to the Magic Mirror. "Mirror, what other dumb jokes has Haraz played?"

The Magic Mirror squirted apple juice all over her face and the front of her dress.

"Ooooohh!" The Queen whirled around. "Florts and collibots! I know who's responsible for that!"

Prince Haraz tried to look sorry, but it was too late.

"That does it!" said the Genie King. "Lamp duty for you, you rascal! One thousand years of service to a lamp." He turned to the Queen. "How's that, my dear?"

"Make it two thousand," said the Queen, drying her face.

Chapter One

Prince Haraz

Almost a year had passed since Stanley Lambchop had gotten over being flat, which he had become when his big bulletin board had settled on him during the night. It had been a pleasant, restful time for all the Lambchops, as this particular evening was.

Dinner was over. In the living room, Mr. Lambchop looked up from his newspaper. "How nice this is, my dear," he said to Mrs. Lambchop, who was darning socks. "I am enjoying my paper and your company, and our boys are studying in their room."

"Let us hope they are," said Mrs. Lambchop. "So often, George, they find excuses not to work."

Mr. Lambchop chuckled. "They *are* imaginative," he said.

In their bedroom, Stanley and his younger brother, Arthur, *were* doing homework. They wore pajamas, and over his Arthur also wore his Mighty Man T-shirt, which helped him to concentrate.

On the desk between them was what they supposed to be a teapot—a round, rather squashed-down pot with a curving spout, and a knob on top for lifting. A wave had rolled it up onto the beach that summer, right to

Stanley's feet; and since Mrs. Lambchop was very fond of old furniture and silverware, he had saved it as a gift for her birthday, now only a week away.

The pot was painted dark green, but streaks of brownish metal showed through. To see if polishing would make it shine, Stanley rubbed the knob with his pajama sleeve.

Puff! Black smoke came from the spout.

"Yipe!" said Arthur. "It's going to explode!"

"Teapots don't explode." Stanley rubbed again. "I just—"

Puff! Puff! Puff! They came rapidly now, joining to form a small cloud in the air above the desk.

"Look out!" Arthur shouted. "Double yipes!"

The black cloud swirled, its blackness becoming a mixture of brown and blue, and began to lose its cloud shape. Arms appeared, and legs, and a head.

"Ready or not, here I come!" said a clear young voice.

Now the cloud was completely gone, and a slender, cheerful-looking boy hovered in the air above the desk. He wore a sort of decorated towel on his head, a loose blue shirt, and curious, flapping brown trousers, one leg of which had snagged on the pot's spout.

"Florts!" said the boy, shaking his leg. "Collibots! I got the puffs right, and the scary cloud, but— There!" Unsnagged, he floated down to the floor and bowed to Stanley and Arthur.

"Who rubbed?" he asked.

Neither of the brothers could speak.

"Well, *someone* did. Genies don't just drop in, you know." The boy bowed again. "How do you do? I am Prince Fawzi Mustafa Aslan Mirza Melek Namerd Haraz. Call me Prince Haraz."

Arthur gasped and dived under his bed.

"What's the matter with him?" the genie asked. "And who are you, and where am I?"

"I'm Stanley Lambchop, and this is the United States of America," Stanley said. "That's Arthur under the bed."

"Not a very friendly welcome," said Prince Haraz. "Especially for someone who's been cooped up in a lamp." He rubbed the back of his neck. "Florts! One thousand years, with my knees right up against my chin. This is my first time out."

"I must have gone crazy," said Arthur from under the bed. "I am just going to lie here until a doctor comes."

"Actually, Prince Haraz, you're here by accident," Stanley said. "I didn't even know that pot was a lamp. Was it the rubbing? Those puffs of smoke, I mean, that turned into you?"

"Were you scared?" The genie laughed. "Just a few puffs, I thought, and I'll *whoooosh* up the spout."

"Scaring *me* wasn't fair," said Arthur, staying under the bed. "I just live in this room because Stanley's my brother. It's his lamp, and he's the one who rubbed it."

"Then he's the one I grant wishes for,"

said Prince Haraz. "Too bad for you."

"I don't care," said Arthur, but he did.

"Can I wish for anything?" Stanley asked. "Anything at all?"

"Not if it's cruel or evil, or really nasty," said Prince Haraz. "I'm a lamp genie, you see, and we're the good kind. Not like those big jar genies. They're stinkers."

"Wish for something, Stanley." Arthur sounded suspicious. "Test him out."

"I'll be right back," Stanley said, and went into the living room.

"Hey!" he said to Mr. and Mrs. Lambchop. "Guess what?"

"Hay is for horses, Stanley, not people," Mr. Lambchop said from behind his newspaper. "Try to remember that."

"Excuse me," Stanley said. "But you'll never guess—"

"My guess is that you and Arthur have not yet finished your homework," said Mrs. Lambchop, looking up from her mending.

"We were doing it," said Stanley, talking very fast, "but I have this pot that turned out to be a lamp, and when I rubbed it, smoke came out, and then a genie, and he says I can wish for things, only I thought I should ask you first. Arthur got scared, so he's hiding under the bed."

Mr. Lambchop chuckled. "When your studying is done, my boy," he said. "But no treasure chests full of gold and diamonds, please. Think of the taxes we would pay!"

"There is your answer, Stanley," said Mrs.

Lambchop. "Now back to work, please."

"Okay, then," said Stanley, going out.

Mrs. Lambchop laughed. "Treasure chests, indeed! Taxes! George, you are very amusing."

Behind his newspaper, Mr. Lambchop smiled again. "Thank you, my dear," he said.

Chapter Two

The Askit Basket

"I told them, but they didn't believe me," Stanley said, back in the bedroom.

"Of course they didn't." Arthur was still under the bed. "Who'd believe a whole person could puff out of a pot?"

"It's not a *pot*," said Prince Haraz. "Now please come out. I apologize for the puffs."

Arthur crawled from under the bed. "No more scary stuff?"

"I promise," the genie said, and they shook hands.

Arthur could hardly wait now. "Stanley! Try a wish!"

"We can't," Stanley said. "Not till our homework is done."

"What's homework?" asked Prince Haraz.

The brothers stared at him, amazed, and then Stanley explained. The genie shook his head.

"*After* schooltime, when you could be having fun?" he said. "Where I come from, we just let Askit Baskets do the work."

"Well, whatever *they* are, I wish I had one," said Stanley, forgetting he was not supposed to wish.

Prince Haraz laughed. "Oh? Look behind you."

Turning, Stanley and Arthur saw a large

straw basket, about the size of a beach ball and decorated with red and green zigzag stripes, floating in the air above the desk.

"Yipes!" said Arthur. "More scary stuff!"

"Don't be silly," said the genie. "It's a perfectly ordinary Askit Basket. Whatever you want to know, Stanley, just ask it."

Feeling rather foolish, Stanley leaned forward and spoke to the basket. "I, uh . . . that is . . . uh . . . Can I have the answers for my math homework? It's the problems on page twenty of my book."

The basket made a steady *huuuummmm* sound, and then a man's voice rose from it, deep and rich like a TV announcer's.

"Thank you for calling Askit Basket," it said. "We're sorry, but all our Answer Genies are busy at this time. Your questions will be answered by the first available personnel. While you wait, enjoy a selection by the Genie-ettes."

Stanley stared at the Askit Basket. Music was coming out of it now, the sort of soft, faraway music he had heard in the elevators of big office buildings.

Prince Haraz shrugged. "What can you do? It's a very popular service."

There was a *click* and the music stopped. Now a female voice, full of bouncy good cheer, came from the basket. "Hi! This is Shireen! Thanks a whole bunch for waiting, and I would like at this time to give you your answers. The first answer is: 5 pears, 6 apples, 8 bananas. The second answer is: Tom is 4

years old, Tim is 7, Ted is 11. The third—"

"Wait!" Stanley shouted. "I can't remember all this!"

"A written record, created especially for

your convenience, is in the basket, sir," said the cheery voice. "Thanks for calling Askit Basket, and have a real nice day!"

Lifting the lid of the basket, Stanley saw a sheet of paper with all his answers on it. "Oh, good!" he said. "Thank you. Can my brother talk now, please?"

Arthur cleared his throat. "Hello, Shireen," he said. "This is Arthur Lambchop speaking. For English, I'm supposed to write about 'What I Want to Be.'"

"Certainly, Mr. Lambchop," said the basket. "Just a teeny moment now, to make sure the handwriting— There! All done!"

Arthur opened the basket and found a sheet of lined paper covered with his own handwriting. He read it aloud.

WHAT I WANT TO BE

by Arthur Lambchop

When I grow up, I want to be President of the United States so that I can make a law not to have any more wars. And get to meet Astronauts. And I would like not to have to go out with girls who want to get all dressed up. Most of all I would like to be the strongest man in the world, like Mighty Man, not to hurt people, but so everybody would be extra nice to me.

The End

Arthur smiled. "That's fine!" he said. "Just what I wanted to say, Shireen."

"Good," said the Basket. "'Bye now! Have a super day!"

The brothers called good-bye, and Prince Haraz plucked the basket out of the air and set it on the desk by his lamp.

"There! Homework's done," he said. "That was a very ordinary sort of wish, Stanley. Isn't there anything special you've always wanted? Something exciting?"

Stanley knew right away what he wanted most. He had always loved animals; how exciting it would be to have his own zoo! But that would take up too much space, he thought. Just one animal then, a truly unusual pet. A lion? Yes! What fun it would be to walk down the street with a pet lion on a leash!

"I wish for a lion!" he said. "Real, but friendly."

"Real, but friendly," said the genie. "No problem."

Stanley realized suddenly that a lion would scare people, and that an elephant would be even greater fun.

"An elephant, I mean!" he shouted. "Not a lion. An elephant!"

"What?" said Prince Haraz. "An eleph—? Oh, collibots! Look what you made me do!"

A most unusual head had formed in the air across the room, a head with an elephant's trunk for a nose but with small, neat, lionlike ears. There was a lion's mane behind the head, but then came an elephant's body and legs in a brownish-gold lion color, and finally a little gray elephant tail with a pretty gold ruff at the tip. All together, these parts made an animal about the size of a medium lion or a small elephant.

"My goodness!" said Stanley. "What's that?"

"A liophant." Prince Haraz seemed annoyed. "It's your fault, not mine. You overlapped your wish."

The liophant opened his mouth wide, gave a half roar, half snort *Grrowll-HONK!* that made them all jump, then sat back on his hind legs and went *pant-pant* like a puppy, looking quite nice.

"Well, we got the friendly part right," said the genie. "The young ones mostly are."

Stanley patted him, and Arthur tickled behind the neat little ears. The liophant licked their hands and Stanley was not at all sorry that he had mixed up his wish.

Just then, a knock sounded on the bedroom door, and Mrs. Lambchop's voice called out, "Homework done?"

"Come in," said Stanley, not thinking, and the door opened.

"How very quiet you—" Mrs. Lambchop began, and then she stopped. Her eyes moved slowly about the room from Prince Haraz to the Askit Basket, and on to the liophant.

"Gracious!" she said.

Prince Haraz made a little bow. "How do you do? You are the mother of these fine lads, yes?"

"I am, thank you," said Mrs. Lambchop. "Have we met? I don't seem to—"

"This is Prince Haraz," Stanley said. "And that's a liophant, and that's an Askit Basket."

"Guess what," said Arthur. "Prince Haraz is a genie, and Stanley can wish for anything he wants."

"How very generous!" Mrs. Lambchop said. "But I'm not sure . . ." Turning, she called into the living room. "George, come here! Something quite unexpected has happened."

"In a moment," Mr. Lambchop called back. "I am reading an unusual story in my newspaper, about a duck who watches TV."

"This is even more unusual that that," she said, and Mr. Lambchop came at once.

"Ah, yes," he said, looking about the room. "Yes, I see. Would someone care to explain?"

"I tried to before," Stanley said. "Remember? About—"

"Wait, dear," said Mrs. Lambchop.

The liophant had been making snuffling, hungry sounds, so she went off to the kitchen and returned with a large bowl full

of hamburger mixed with warm milk. While the liophant ate, Stanley told his parents what had happened.

Mr. Lambchop thought for a moment. "Unusual indeed," he said. "And what a fine opportunity for you, Stanley. But I do not approve of using the Askit Basket for your homework, boys. Nor will your teachers, I'm afraid."

"My plan is, let's not tell them," Arthur said.

Mr. Lambchop gave him a long look. "Would you take credit for work you have not done?"

Arthur blushed. "Oh! Well, I guess not . . . I wasn't thinking. Because of all the excitement, you know?"

Mr. Lambchop wrote NOT IN USE on a piece of cardboard and taped it to the Askit Basket.

"It is too late for more wishing tonight," Mrs. Lambchop said. "Prince Haraz, there is a folding cot in the closet, so you will be comfortable here. Tomorrow is Saturday, which we always spend together in the park. You will join us, yes?"

"Thank you very much," said the genie, and he helped Stanley and Arthur set up the cot.

The liophant was already asleep, and Mrs. Lambchop picked up his bowl. "Gracious! Three pounds of the best hamburger, and he ate every bit." She put out the light. "Good night to you all."

It was quite dark in the bedroom, but

some moonlight shone through the window. From their beds, Stanley and Arthur could see that Prince Haraz was still sitting up in his cot. For a moment all was silence except for the gentle snoring of the liophant, and then the genie said, "Sorry about the snoring. It's having all that nose, probably."

"It's okay," Arthur said sleepily. "Do genies snore?"

"We don't even sleep," said Prince Haraz. "Your mother was so kind, I didn't want to tell her. She might have felt bad."

"I'll try to stay awake, if you want to talk," Stanley said.

"No thanks," said the genie. "I'll be fine. After all those years alone in the lamp, it's nice just having company."

Chapter Three

In the Park

Everyone slept late and enjoyed a large breakfast, particularly the liophant, who ate two more pounds of hamburger, five bananas, and three loaves of bread.

Then, since all the Lambchops enjoyed tennis, they set out with their rackets for the courts in the big park close by. Aware that his genie clothes would puzzle people, Prince Haraz borrowed slacks and a shirt from Stanley, and came along.

In the street, they met Ralph Jones, an old college friend of Mr. Lambchop's, whom they had not seen for quite some time.

"Nice running into you, George, and you too, Mrs. Lambchop," said Mr. Jones. "Hello, Arthur. Hello, Stanley. Aren't you the one who was flat? Rounded out nicely, I see."

"You always did have a fine memory, Ralph," Mr. Lambchop said. "Let me introduce our houseguest, Prince Haraz. He is a foreign student, here to study our ways."

"How do you do?" said the genie. "I am Fawzi Mustafa Aslan Mirza Melek Namerd Haraz."

"How do you do?" Mr. Jones said. "Well, I must be off. Good-bye, Lambchops. Nice to have met you, Prince Fawzi Mustafa

Aslan Mirza Melek Namerd Haraz."

"He *does* have a wonderful memory," Mrs. Lambchop said as Mr. Jones walked away.

They set out for the park again.

"How it would surprise Mr. Jones to learn that Prince Haraz was a genie," Mrs. Lambchop remarked. "The whole world would be amazed. Gracious! We'd all be famous, I'm sure."

"I was famous once, when I was flat," Stanley said. "I didn't like it after a while."

"I remember," said Mrs. Lambchop. "Nevertheless, I wish I knew myself what being famous feels like."

Prince Haraz looked at Stanley in a questioning way, and Stanley gave a little nod. The genie smiled and nodded back.

They were just passing the Famous Museum of Art, one of the city's most important buildings. A tour bus, filled with visitors from foreign countries, had stopped before the museum, and a guide was lecturing the passengers through a megaphone.

"Over where those trees are, that's our great City Park!" he announced. "Here, on the right, is the Famous Museum of Art, full of great paintings and statues and— Oh, what a surprise! We're in luck today, folks! That's Mrs. George Lambchop, coming right toward us! Harriet Lambchop herself, in person! Right there, with the tennis racket!"

The tourists cried out in pleased astonishment, turning in their seats to stare where the guide was pointing.

"What—? He means *you*, Harriet!" said Mr. Lambchop.

"I think so," said Mrs. Lambchop. "Oh, my goodness! They're coming!"

The tourists were rushing from the bus. A Japanese family reached Mrs. Lambchop first, all with cameras.

"Please, Lambchop lady," said the husband, bowing politely. "Honor to take picture, yes?"

"Of course," said Mrs. Lambchop. "I hope you are enjoying our country. But why *my* picture? I'm not—"

"No, no! Famous, famous! Famous Lambchop lady!" cried the Japanese family, taking pictures as fast as they could.

Mrs. Lambchop understood suddenly that

her wish had been granted. "Thank you, Prince Haraz!" she said. "What fun!"

She posed graciously for all the tourists and signed dozens of autographs. In the park she was recognized again, and had to do more posing and signing.

It was now midmorning, and all the park's tennis courts were occupied, but the Lambchops' disappointment lessened when they saw a crowd gathered by one court and learned that Tom McRude, the world's best tennis player, was about to lecture and demonstrate his strokes. Tom McRude was known for his terrible temper and bad manners, but the Lambchops were eager to see him nevertheless. With Prince Haraz, they squeezed close to the court, next to the TV-news cameras covering the event.

"None of you can ever be a great tennis player like me," Tom McRude was saying. "But at least you can have the thrill of seeing me."

A little old lady in the crowd gave a tiny sneeze, and he glared at her. "What's the matter with you, granny?"

The old lady burst into tears, and friends led her away.

"What a mean fellow!" Prince Haraz whispered to Stanley.

"I can't stand old sneezing people!" said Tom McRude. "Okay, now I'll show how I hit my great forehand! First—"

"Hold it, Tom!" called the TV-news director. "We've just spotted Harriet Lambchop here. What a break! Maybe she'll say a few words for our cameras!"

Even Tom McRude was impressed. "*The* Harriet Lambchop? Wow!"

"Swing those cameras this way, fellows!" The director ran over to Mrs. Lambchop, holding out a microphone.

"Wonderful to see you!" he said. "Everybody wants to know your views. Favorite color? What about the foreign situation? Do you sleep in pajamas or a nightgown?"

"Isn't that rather personal?" asked Mr. Lambchop.

"George, please. . . ." Mrs. Lambchop spoke into the microphone. "Thank you all for your kind welcome," she said. "I would just like to say that I'm glad my fans are having such a lovely day in this delightful park."

The crowd cheered and waved, and Mrs. Lambchop waved back and blew kisses. Jealous of the attention she was getting, Tom McRude whacked a tennis ball over the fence behind him.

Noticing, Mrs. Lambchop spoke again into the microphone. "And now, let us give this great champion our attention!"

"Yeah!" growled Tom McRude. When the TV cameras had swung back to him, he went on. "I need a volunteer, so that I can demonstrate how terrible most players are compared to me!"

Mr. Lambchop thought it would be thrilling to share a court with a champion. Signaling with his racket, he stepped forward.

Tom McRude handed him some balls. "Okay, try a serve."

Mr. Lambchop prepared to serve.

"He's got his feet wrong!" Tom McRude shouted. "And his grip is wrong! Everything is wrong!"

This made Mr. Lambchop so nervous that he served two balls into the net instead of over it.

"Terrible! Terrible! Watch how I do it," said Tom McRude, running to the far side of the court. From there he served five balls, so hard and fast that Mr. Lambchop missed the first four entirely. The fifth one knocked the racket out of his hand.

"Ha, ha!" laughed Tom McRude. "Now let's see you run!"

He began hitting whizzing forehands and backhands at sharp angles across the court, making Mr. Lambchop look foolish as he raced back and forth, getting very red in the face and missing practically every shot.

The other Lambchops grew angry, as did Prince Haraz. "This need not continue, you know," he whispered to Stanley.

Just then, Mr. Lambchop came skidding to a halt before them, banging his knee with his racket as he missed yet another of the champion's powerful shots.

"Ha, ha! This is how *I* give lessons!" shouted Tom McRude.

Mr. Lambchop looked at Stanley, then at Prince Haraz. "Okay," Stanley said, and the genie smiled a little smile.

"Thank you," said Mr. Lambchop. Returning to the court, he called out to the crowd. "Ladies and gentlemen, I will try my serve again!"

Across the net, Tom McRude gave a nasty laugh and slashed his big racket through the air.

Mr. Lambchop served a ball, not into the net this time, but fast as a bullet right where it was supposed to go. Tom McRude's mouth fell open as the ball whizzed past him. "Out!" he shouted. "That ball was out!"

Voices rose from the crowd. "Shame on you! . . . The ball was *in*! . . . What a liar! . . . In, in, in!"

Tom McRude shook his fist. "I'll bet you can't do that again!"

Mr. Lambchop served three more balls, each even faster than the first one, and as perfectly placed. Tom McRude could not even touch them, though the last one bounced up into his nose.

Then Mr. Lambchop rallied with him, gliding swiftly about the court and returning every shot with ease. With powerful forehands, he made Tom McRude run from corner to corner; with little drop shots, he drew the champion up to the net, then lobbed high shots to send him racing back again. Nobody has ever played such great tennis as Mr. Lambchop played that day.

Tom McRude was soon too tired, and too angry, to continue. He threw down his racket and jumped on it.

"You're just lucky!" he yelled. "Besides, I have a cold! And the sun was in my eyes the whole time!" Pushing his way through the crowd, he ran out of the park.

There was tremendous cheering for Mr. Lambchop, who just smiled modestly and waved his racket in a friendly way. Then he came over to where the other Lambchops and Prince Haraz were standing with the TV-news director.

"You're really *good*," the director said. "Frankly, you looked terrible when you first went out there."

"It takes me a while to get warmed up," Mr. Lambchop said, and led his family away.

Leaving the park, Mrs. Lambchop signed many more autographs, and a reporter from *Famous Faces* magazine was waiting to interview her at home.

"You'll be on the cover of our next issue," said the reporter. "How much do you weigh?

Will there be a movie about your life? Who gave you your first kiss?"

"None of your business!" said Mr. Lambchop, and the reporter went away.

They watched the evening news on television, hoping Mr. Lambchop's tennis would be shown, but only Mrs. Lambchop appeared, with Tom McRude in the background. "The celebrated Harriet Lambchop was in the park today," said the newscaster, after which came a close-up of Mrs. Lambchop saying, "I'm glad my fans are having such a lovely day," and that was that.

Dinner was interrupted several times by phone calls for Mrs. Lambchop from newspaper and television people. The calls bothered Mr. Lambchop, but not the liophant, who ate four pork chops, a jar of peanut butter, a quart of potato salad, and the rubber mat from under his dish.

Chapter Four

The Brothers Fly

"I'm not complaining," said Arthur, complaining, "but it's not fair. Some people have liophants, or get famous. I want to be President, or as strong as Mighty Man, but all I got was one minute with an Askit Basket we can't even use anymore."

It was after dinner, and the brothers were in their bedroom with Prince Haraz, all in pajamas.

"It's not my fault, Arthur." The genie

looked hurt. "I just follow orders. Rub, I appear. Wish, I grant. That's it."

Stanley felt sorry for his brother. "I don't think you should be President, Arthur," he said. "But I'll wish for you to be the strongest man in the world. I wish it, Prince Haraz!"

"Oh, good!" said Arthur.

He waited, but nothing happened. "Darn! It didn't work!" Disappointed, he punched his left hand with his right fist.

"Owwww!" Jumping up and down, Arthur flapped his hand to relieve the pain.

"When you're the strongest man in the world," said Prince Haraz, "you have to be careful what you hit."

"But I still feel like me," Arthur said. Testing himself, he took hold of the big desk with one hand and lifted it easily above his head.

Stanley's mouth flew open, and so did the desk drawers.

Pencils, marbles, and paper clips rained down onto the floor.

"Ooops!" said Arthur.

"This is ridiculous," said Prince Haraz, helping him tidy up. "The strongest man in the world, in a bedroom picking up desks! Out having adventures, that's where you should be."

"We can't now," Arthur said. "It's almost bedtime."

Stanley had an idea. "There'd be time if we could fly! Can't we all fly somewhere?"

"I've always been able to," said the genie. "For you two, it'll take wishing."

"I wish!" shouted Stanley. "Flying! Arthur and me both!"

For a moment the brothers held their breath, expecting to be swept up into the air. Then Arthur tried small flapping movements with his elbows.

"Oh, collibots!" said the genie. "Not like that. Just *think* of flying, and where you want to go."

It worked.

Stanley and Arthur found themselves suddenly a few feet off the floor, face down and quite comfortable, and however they wished to go, up or down, forward or back, was how they went. It was like swimming in soft, invisible water, but without the effort of swimming. Prince Haraz gave advice as the brothers glided happily about the room: "Point your toes. . . . Heads up! . . . Good, very good. . . . Yes, I think you're ready now!"

He opened a window and leaned out. "Hmmm. . . . This breeze may be coolish higher up. We'd better wear something extra."

Stanley and Arthur put on bathrobes and gloves, and the genie chose a red parka and a dragon-face ski mask. Then he said, "Away we go!" and the brothers floated through the window after him, out into the night.

Up! Up! UP! they went, leveling off now and then to practice speeding, but mostly

rising steadily higher. Stanley and Arthur
flew side by side, gaining confidence from
each other, and the genie kept an eye on
them from behind.

It was a beautiful night. The sky above
them was full of stars. Below them the lights
of the city twinkled as brightly as the stars.

The brothers' white bathrobes and the genie's red parka, shone in the moonlight.

They flew above the big park, where an orchestra was giving a concert. Music floated up to them: the clear, sweet tones of flutes and violins and trumpets; the deep, strong notes of cymbals and drums.

"Oh, I'm enjoying this!" Prince Haraz called through his dragon mask. "So different from inside that lamp!"

The three fliers joined hands and circled the blaze of light from where the orchestra sat. It was like ice-skating to music at a rink, but much more fun.

In the distance, the wing lights of a big airplane blinked across the sky.

"Let's chase it!" Stanley shouted.

Prince Haraz laughed. "Go on ! I'll catch up!"

Whooooosh! Whooooosh! Holding their arms by their sides, Stanley and Arthur flashed like rockets across the sky, their bathrobes flapping like the sails of a boat. The big airplane was fast, but the brothers were faster. Catching up, they flew around and around it, looking through the windows at the passengers reading and eating from tiny trays.

Arthur saw a little girl with a comic book. Zooming close to her window, he stretched his neck, trying to read over her shoulder. The little girl looked up and saw him. Being mean, she held the comic book down where he couldn't see it, and stuck out her tongue.

Arthur stuck his tongue out at her, and the little girl scowled and pulled a curtain across her window.

On the other side of the plane, Stanley

saw a very tired-looking young couple with a crying baby across their laps, keeping them awake. Flying up next to the window so that the baby could see him, he made a funny face, puffing his lips and wrinkling his nose. The baby smiled, and Stanley put his thumbs in his ears and wriggled his other fingers. The baby smiled again, and went to sleep.

Stanley flew back around the plane, past the cockpit, to join Arthur on the other side.

There were two pilots in the cockpit, and one saw Stanley fly by. Turning his head, he now saw both brothers hovering above a wing tip, waiting for Prince Haraz to catch up.

"Guess what I see out there, Bert," he said.

"The stars in the sky, Tom, and below us the mighty ocean," replied the other pilot.

"No," said Tom. "Two kids in bathrobes."

"Ha, Ha! What a joker!" said Bert, but he turned to look.

Only Prince Haraz could be seen now above the wing, his parka flapping as he looked around for Stanley and Arthur, who were hiding from him behind the plane.

"So what do you see, Bert?" asked Tom, keeping his own eyes straight ahead. "Two kids in bathrobes, right?"

"Wrong," said Bert quietly. "I see a guy in ski clothes, with a dragon face."

The pilots stared at each other, then out

at the wing again, but the genie had flown to join the brothers behind the plane.

"Nobody there," said Tom. "Let's never mention this to anyone, Bert. Okay?

"Good idea," said Bert. "Definitely."

They flew on and had nothing more to say.

A giant ocean liner, ablaze with lights, made its way across the sea below.

"Come on!" Arthur shouted, whizzing away with Stanley behind him. Again, Prince Haraz laughed and let them go.

The beauty of the great ship made the brothers marvel as they drew near. It was like an enormous birthday cake, each deck a layer sparkling with the brightness of a thousand candles.

"Look, Stanley!" Arthur cried. "They're having a party on the main deck!"

They flew closer to enjoy the fun and saw then that it was not a party, but a robbery.

The main deck was crowded because robbers had lined up all the passengers and were taking their money and jewelry. The helicopter in which the robbers had arrived was parked close by, below the captain's bridge. The captain and his fellow officers had struggled, but they were chained up now on the bridge.

"We've got to do something, Stanley!" Arthur said.

Zooming down to the bridge, he shouted over the railing at the robbers below. "Stop, you crooks! Give back all that money and jewelry and stuff!"

Using his great strength, Arthur tore away the ropes and chains that bound the ship's officers. It was as if he were just tearing paper.

Amazed, the robbers stumbled backward, dropping money and jewelry all over the deck.

"Oh, lordy!" one robber yelled. "Who are you?"

Remembering his favorite comic-book hero, Arthur could not resist showing off. He flew ten feet up in the air and stayed there, looking fierce.

"I am Mighty Arthur!" he shouted in a deep voice. "Mighty Arthur, Enemy of Crime!"

Exclamations rose from the robbers and

passengers and ship's officers. "So strong, and a flyer too! . . . Who expected Mighty Arthur? . . . Are we ever *lucky*! . . . This ought to be on TV!"

Now Stanley swooped down from the sky with his bathrobe belt untied, so that his robe flared behind him like a cape. "I'm Mighty Stanley!" he called. "Defender of the Innocent!"

"I do that too!" Arthur cried, wishing he had made *his* robe a cape. "We both do good things, but I'm the really strong one!"

He saw suddenly that several robbers were trying to escape in the helicopter. It was already rising, but Arthur flashed through the air until he was directly above it, and with one hand pushed it back down onto the

deck. When the frightened robbers jumped out, the ship's officers grabbed them and tied them up.

Now the passengers were even more amazed. "Did you see that?" they said, and "Mighty Arthur and Mighty Stanley, both on the same day!" and "This is *better* than TV!"

The brothers flew up to join Prince Haraz, who had been circling over the ship. "What a pair of show-offs!" said the genie. "Even worse than I used to be."

As they set out for home, the cheers of the grateful passengers and crew floated up behind them. "Hooray for our rescuers!" they heard, and "Especially Mighty Arthur!" and a moment later, "Mighty Stanley too, of course!"

Soon the big ship was no more than an outline of tiny lights in the black sea below, and the last cheer was only a whisper above the rushing of the wind: "Three cheers . . . for . . . the Enemy . . . of . . . Crime . . . and the . . . Defender . . . of the . . . Inno . . . cent!"

The brothers felt very proud, but it had been a tiring adventure, and they were not sorry when the city came into sight.

Chapter Five

The Last Wish

Flying back into the bedroom, the three adventurers found Mr. and Mrs. Lambchop waiting anxiously. The liophant, who had just finished an enormous bowl of spaghetti mixed with chocolate cookies and milk, was asleep.

"Thank goodness!" Mrs. Lambchop ran to hug her sons.

"Where have you been?" Mr. Lambchop was stern. "Is that you, Prince Haraz, behind that dragon face?"

The genie took off his mask. "Were you worried? Sorry. We went for a little flight."

"Wait till you hear!" said Arthur. "You can't tell from looking, but I'm the strongest man in the world, and—"

"Take off those robes and gloves," said Mrs. Lambchop. "It is not wise to get over-heated."

She went on, as they put their things away. "*Such* an evening! The phone never stopped. I was asked to go on four TV shows, and to advertise a new soap—they wanted to photograph me in the bathtub, so of course I said no!—and then, to find the window open and the three of you *gone*! Such a fright!"

"We thought we'd be right back," said Stanley, apologizing. "We didn't know so many exciting things would happen."

Everybody sat down, and Stanley told about wishing Arthur strong, and the flying, and chasing the airplane, and the robbers on the ship. Mr. and Mrs. Lambchop both gave deep sighs when Stanley was done.

"It seems, Prince Haraz," Mr. Lambchop said, "that there are often unexpected consequences when wishes come true."

"Oh, yes," said the genie. "That's what got me into a lamp."

"It's not just the Askit Basket problem," Mr. Lambchop said. "Mrs. Lambchop has been famous less than a day, and already she is exhausted and has lost all her privacy. And though Tom McRude deserved what he got, his tennis comes from natural ability. I am not proud of having shamed him by using magic."

"And Arthur's great strength will make other boys afraid of him," Mrs. Lambchop said. "And flying, mixing with criminals . . . Dear me! We must consider all this. I will make hot chocolate. It is helpful when there is serious thinking to be done."

Everyone enjoyed the delicious hot chocolate she brought from the kitchen, with a marshmallow for each cup. The Lambchops sat quietly, sipping and thinking. Prince Haraz, having said twice that he was sorry to have caused problems, began to pace up and down. The liophant was still asleep.

At last Mr. Lambchop put down his cup and cleared his throat. "Your attention, please," he said, and they all looked at him.

"Here is my opinion," he said. "Genies and their magic, Prince Haraz, are fine for faraway lands and long-ago times, but the Lambchops have always been quite natural people, and this is the United States of America, and the time is today. We are grateful for the excitement you have offered, but now I must ask: Is it possible for Stanley to *un*wish all the wishes he has made?"

"It is, actually," said the genie.

"How clever of you, George!" cried Mrs. Lambchop.

Arthur sighed. "I don't know. . . . I really like the flying. But being so strong, I guess nobody *would* play with me."

"I care most about the liophant," Stanley said. "Couldn't we just keep him?"

"He is very lovable," said Mrs. Lambchop. "But he never stops eating! We cannot *afford* to keep him."

"Sad, but true," Mr. Lambchop said. "Now please tell us, Prince Haraz, what must be done."

"It's called Reverse Wishing." The genie took the little green lamp from the desk and turned it over. "The instructions should be right here on the bottom. Let's see. . . ."

He studied the words carved into the bottom of the lamp. "Seems simple enough. Each wish has to be separately reversed. I just say 'Mandrono!' and—" His voice rose. "Oh, collibots! Double florts! See that little circle there? This is a *training* lamp! There may not be enough wishes left!"

"A training lamp?" exclaimed Mr. Lambchop. "What is that?"

"They're for beginners like me, so we don't overdo for one person," Prince Haraz said unhappily. "The little 'fifteen' in the circle, that's all the wishes I'm allowed for Stanley."

The Lambchops all spoke at once. "What? . . . You never told us! . . . Only fifteen? . . . Oh, dear!"

"Please, I'm embarrassed enough," said the genie, very red in the face. "A *training* lamp! As if I were a baby!"

"We are all beginners at one time or another," said Mr. Lambchop. "What matters is, are fifteen wishes enough?"

The genie counted on his fingers to be

sure he got it right. "Askit Basket, liophant—lucky he doesn't count double!—that's two, and fame for Mrs. Lambchop and the fancy tennis, that's four. Making Arthur strong is five, flying for him *and* Stanley is two more . . ." He smiled. "Seven, and seven for reversing is fourteen! One wish left over for some sort of good-bye treat!"

"Thank goodness!" Mrs. Lambchop hesitated. "It is very late. . . . Could you begin the reversing *now*, do you think?"

Prince Haraz nodded. "I'll do the whole family in a bunch. Let's see . . . Strength, famous, tennis, two flying. Ready, Arthur? No more Mighty Man after this, I'm afraid."

"Will I feel weak?" Arthur asked. "Will I flop over?"

The genie shook his head. "Mandrono!" he said. "Mandrono, Mandrono, Mandrono, Mandrono!"

Arthur felt a prickling on the back of his neck. When the prickling stopped, he gave the big desk a shove, but couldn't budge it.

"I'm just regular me again," he said. "Oh, well."

"And I am just Harriet Lambchop again," said Mrs. Lambchop, smiling. "An unimportant person."

"To all of us, my dear, you are the most important person we know," said Mr. Lambchop. "Arthur, you are as strong as you were yesterday. Think of it that way."

The genie sipped the last of his hot chocolate. "Where was I? Oh, yes . . ." He glanced at the Askit Basket. "Mandrono!" The basket vanished. "Just the liophant now," he said.

Everyone looked at the liophant, who was sitting up now in the corner, scratching behind his lion ears with his elephant trunk. Stanley patted him, and the liophant licked his hand.

"How sweet!" Mrs. Lambchop said. "George, perhaps . . . ?"

"What makes liophants truly happy," said the genie, "is open-spaces, and the company of other liophants."

"Then send him where it's like that," Stanley said bravely, patting again. The liophant vanished halfway through the pat.

For a moment no one spoke.

"Good for you, Stanley," Mr. Lambchop

said softly. "And now you must think of a
last wish to make."

While Stanley thought, Mrs. Lambchop collected the hot chocolate cups. "Where will you go now, Prince Haraz?" she said.

"Back into that stuffy little lamp," said the genie. "And then it's wait, wait, wait! Hundreds and hundreds of years, probably. It's my punishment for playing too many tricks. My friends warned me, but I wouldn't listen."

He sighed. "Mosef, Ali, Ben Sifa, little Fawz. Such wonderful fellows! I think of them when I'm alone in the lamp, the *fun* they must be having. The games, the freedom . . . ." His voice trembled, and the Lambchops felt very sorry for him.

Suddenly, Arthur had an idea. He whispered it to Stanley.

"Why the whispering?" the genie said

crossly. "Let's have that last wish, Stanley, and I'll smoke back into my lamp."

The brothers were smiling at each other. "Good idea, right?" said Arthur.

"Oh, yes!" Stanley turned to the genie. "Here is my last wish, Prince Haraz. I wish for you *not* to stay in the lamp, but to go back where you came from, to be with your genie friends and have good times with them, forever from now on!"

Prince Haraz gasped. His mouth fell open.

Mr. Lambchop worried that he might faint. "Are you all right?" he asked. "Is Stanley not allowed to set you free?"

"Yes, yes . . . It's allowed." The genie spoke softly. "But nobody ever used a wish for the sake of a genie. Not until now."

"How selfish people can be!" said Mrs. Lambchop.

Prince Haraz rubbed his eyes. "What a fine family this is," he said, beginning to smile. "I thank you all. The name of Lambchop will be honored always, wherever genies meet."

His smile enormous now, he shook hands with each of the Lambchops. The last shake was with Stanley, and the genie was already a bit smoky about the edges. By the time he let go of Stanley's hand, he was all smoke, a dark cloud that swirled briefly over the little lamp on the desk, then poured in through the spout until not a puff remained.

Full of wonder, the Lambchops gathered about the lamp, and after a moment Arthur put his lips to the spout.

"Good-bye, Prince Haraz!" he called. "Have a nice trip!"

From within the lamp, a faraway voice called back, "Bless you all. . . ." and then there was only silence in the room.

Mr. Lambchop was the first to speak. "I'm proud of you, Stanley," he said. "Your last wish was generous and kind."

"It was my idea, actually," Arthur said, and Mrs. Lambchop kissed the top of his head. "Off to bed now, boys," she said. "Tomorrow is another day."

Stanley and Arthur got into bed, and she turned out the light.

"The lamp was supposed to be a surprise birthday present," Stanley said sleepily. "Now it won't be a surprise at all."

"I will love it anyhow," said Mrs. Lambchop. "And Prince Haraz was a tremendous surprise. Good night, my dears."

She kissed them both, and so did Mr. Lambchop, and they went out.

The brothers lay quietly in the darkness for a while, and then Stanley sighed. "I miss the liophant a bit," he said. "But I don't mind about the rest."

"Me neither." Arthur yawned. "Florts, Stanley, and good night."

"Goodnight," Stanley said. "Collibots."

"Mandrono," murmured Arthur, and soon they were both asleep.

Born in New York City, **Jeff Brown** has been a story editor and assistant film producer in Hollywood. He has worked on the editorial staffs of *The New Yorker* and the *Saturday Evening Post*, and his stories have  appeared in these magazines and many others. Mr. Brown is the author of several other books about the Lambchop family, including FLAT STANLEY and INVISIBLE STANLEY.

 **Steve Björkman** has been drawing since he was a boy, usually during class at school, but only when the teacher was boring. Some teachers told him it would never get him any-where, but it did. Now he gets to draw for children's books, advertising, and greeting cards. He lives in Irvine, California, with his wife, three kids, a dog, a cat, and two tortoises.